D1258311

This book belongs to:

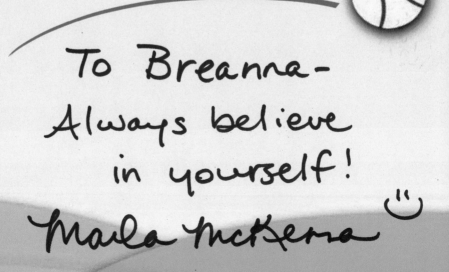

To Breanna—
Always believe
in yourself!

Marla McKenna

Give a dog a home!

Best friends come in all shapes and sizes.
Your new best friend is waiting for you.

To Breanna -
Always believe
in yourself!
:")
Maria Hofferts

Sadie's
BIG
Steal

Marla McKenna

Published by Nico 11 Publishing & Design
Quantity order requests can be emailed to
mike@nico11publishing.com

Author: Marla McKenna
Sadie's Big Steal
www.marlamckenna.com

Illustrations: Alvin jude Behik

ISBN-10:1945907150
ISBN-13:978-1945907159

Sales Categories:

Children's Books | Sports & Outdoors | Baseball
Children's Books | Animals/Dogs
Children's Books | Growing Up | Friends, Social Skills & School Life

Be well read.

Nico 11 Publishing & Design

www.nico11publishing.com

To God,
with Him all things are possible.

To everyone who has supported me
along my journey, my sincere thanks,
especially to my family and close friends.

To all the Mom's Big Catch kids I've
visited across the country who have asked
for and inspired me to write another
book. Thank you for all your warm
smiles, letters, and pictures. Remember
"Don't Give Up on Your Dreams!"

And to all our furry friends we've loved,
lost, and to those still waiting for forever
homes. Your unconditional love is priceless.

Racing and panting, I leaped for my big catch and saved the home run from going over the fence! Clenching the ball, I could only imagine how sweet that special major league baseball up on the shelf would feel between my teeth! It would be mighty tasty I'm sure! I ran the ball back to Ashley and got ready for Julia to bat again. Ashley wound up and threw a fastball to Julia, who waited patiently for her perfect pitch. Julia was quite the slugger!

My pals, Gomer and Gus, liked it when the ball landed in their yard so they could join in the fun. Like me, Gomer and Gus wished we could play with that special ball too. Yes, they knew about it...all the dogs in the neighborhood knew about it. Exciting news like that travels fast!

Ever since Mom's big catch at the stadium, we were the talk of the town. When I first saw that beautiful ball, I just wanted to play with it! My friends all dared me to take it but it was out of my reach up on the shelf. Dad always let Julia and Ashley sleep with it on special occasions. Julia's birthday was tomorrow so I'd finally have my chance! I couldn't wait to tell Gomer and Gus. We had waited so long for this day, and it was finally here. We needed a plan.

Tomorrow would be the night of the big steal!

Morning came quickly and my eyes opened with the shimmering rays of sunshine peeking in Julia's window. The birds filled the air with a cheerful melody.

Today was the day!

I woke up Julia with a big birthday kiss on the cheek, jumped off her bed, and ran out the doggie door to share the fun news with my friends.

We devised a plan. I would wait for Julia to fall asleep and then steal the ball right out from under her. Then I'd quietly sneak the ball outside and bury it in the backyard. When the coast was clear and my family was gone for the day at school and work, I would dig it up. Oh how much fun it would be! We'd play with that amazing ball! This plan was sure to work.

Gomer, a bit concerned, asked, "But what if you get caught and they find out you took it, Sadie?" Other dogs walked by at that time and heard what we were planning.

"Just blame Rosie. Rosie looks different and isn't from around here. She doesn't have family or friends, so no one will even care," they shouted out as they continued on their walk. I didn't really like their idea but I really wanted that ball so it's all I could think about.

The day passed slowly as I gazed out the window waiting for Julia and Ashley to come home from school. I peacefully drifted in and out of my nap. I woke up at the first sound of the giant, yellow bus. I knew as soon as my girls came running through the front door, I'd jump into their arms. Warm hugs always waited for me there!

At that moment, I couldn't help but think about Rosie. I wondered how many hugs she'd ever gotten? All I knew, she was a dog without a home. I would just see her quietly wandering around our neighborhood. Word on the street was she always ran away when anyone tried to get too close. I knew the people at the animal shelter would want to help her, but Rosie didn't know that. I once heard Mom say, "Fear can cause people to run." So I suppose that's why Rosie bolted… she was afraid and didn't know what would happen to her if she trusted people or other dogs. I decided the next time I saw Rosie, I'd be her friend.

It was time to celebrate Julia's birthday!

Everyone had a piece of delicious chocolate cherry cake; that is, everyone but me! I snuck a tiny lick of vanilla ice cream, and then Mom gave me a scrumptious, juicy bone. It was super yummy! Before Julia blew out her candles, she made a wish. I bet she wished Dad would give her the special ball for the night! That's what I'd wish for! My tummy was full, and I was ready to curl up and go to sleep. I needed to get a little rest before my exciting adventure.

But I couldn't fall asleep because I heard Julia talking to Mom and Dad. She told them about her day at school and how they'd recently gotten a new student. Julia liked this new friend but heard other kids calling her names and making fun of her just because she looked and talked a little differently and wasn't from here. That kind of sounded familiar to me...like Rosie. My ears perked up so I wouldn't miss what Mom and Dad told Julia. I barked and Mom petted me behind the ears. She knew how much I loved that. Dad asked Julia, "Do you like this new friend?"

"Yes, I like her very much," Julia said confidently. "She makes me laugh, and I feel like I can tell her all of my secrets, and she'll keep them. We pinky promise."

"That's all that matters, Julia!" said Mom. "It doesn't matter what anyone else says, you have to do what you feel is right in your heart. Don't let anyone change who you are, Julia. You are beautiful inside and out and have many special gifts. I'm sure your new friend is special in her own way too; everyone is." Mom and Dad went on to explain to Julia how important it was not to let other people make you do something you don't want to; how you should stick up for yourself and your friends. Always believe in yourself!

"We are very proud of you, Julia!" said Dad.

Julia hugged Mom and Dad good night. Then Dad surprisingly tossed Julia the ball he was hiding behind his back, and said, "Here you go Julia, Happy Birthday!"

"Yes! My wish came true! Thanks Dad," Julia shouted out happily.

Julia snuggled up close to me and said, "I love you, Sadie girl. You're my best buddy, and we can sleep with our favorite ball tonight. I'm happy to share it with you!" I gave the baseball a big lick, and it felt like magical fireworks exploded inside of me; one of every bright and beautiful color! My heart was so happy!

As Julia and I drifted off to sleep, I realized I could never take away Julia's wish and steal the ball from her tonight. I also realized I could never blame Rosie or anyone else for something I did. I decided I would find Rosie tomorrow. I wanted to be her friend. I'd tell her the people at the animal shelter wanted to help her, and she shouldn't be afraid. It was her only chance of finding a forever home with a family who wanted to adopt and love her. But what would I tell all my friends in the morning? They'd be waiting for me, and I wouldn't have the ball. I could tell them Julia didn't get to sleep with it. No, I would tell them the truth because that was the right thing to do. If they were really my friends, they'd understand.

The sun rose again and morning greeted me with a welcoming smile. I grabbed my leash and eagerly waited to go on my walk with Mom. I was in a hurry that morning and our walk quickly turned into a brisk run as I looked up and down the streets for Rosie. I spotted her and ran faster as Mom tugged on my leash. I was on a mission. When we caught up to Rosie, she was a bit scared. I told her I wanted to be her friend and about the shelter. I saw Mom pet her behind the ears just like she does to me…that's always my favorite. Rosie liked it too. Mom checked for a collar and name tag but there was none. Rosie hesitated but then cautiously came home with us.

Then Mom took her to the animal shelter. I could see Rosie wasn't sure what was going on but I did my best to make her feel better. I told her everything would be okay. When Mom arrived at the shelter, our neighbors were there. They had been thinking of adopting a dog and immediately fell in love with Rosie. Though Rosie looked a little tough on the outside, I knew she had a big heart on the inside. Sometimes you just have to trust what you feel.

I ran outside to tell Gomer and Gus the happy news. They were all waiting for me hoping to play with that special ball. I told them I had stolen something much more important, the heart of friendship. "We're getting a new neighbor and her name is Rosie."

They said, "Rosie? You mean the one those other dogs were talking about who is…"

I stopped them and said, "Who is our new wonderful friend!" When Rosie came outside with her family, you could just see how happy she was getting lots of warm hugs.

What a great day this turned out to be!

Mom opened the gates to our fence in the backyard and everyone welcomed Rosie to our team. We all took our positions in our very own special outfield. It was the best feeling ever! I imagined the fans cheering loudly, the bright lights of the stadium shining down on us and the announcer shouting out those magical words, "Play ball!" I was ready; we all were ready! And we had to be, because Julia was up to bat. We all backed up. Ashley threw her a curveball and Julia hit it harder than I've ever seen. We all ran for the ball and jumped high into the cool, spring breeze anticipating our big catch!

As for that beautiful and perfect major league baseball, it stayed up on the shelf right where it belonged!

Donations:

The mission of the Linda Blair WorldHeart Foundation is to make sure that every animal they rescue is given a second chance at a happy life and a loving forever home. Thank you to all those involved in making this wonderful Foundation possible. Partial proceeds from this book are donated to their cause, with special thanks to Rick Springfield and his family for their generosity in matching this donation. Every dog deserves to be loved, and together we can all make that happen. Thank you for your support!

Made in the USA
Middletown, DE
07 January 2019